ARABIC

CALLIGRAPHY

PRACTICE

BOOK

ARABIC CALLIGRAPHY

Arabic and a number of other languages, such as Persian, Kurdish, Pashto, Urdu, and others, are written using the Arabic alphabet. There are twenty-eight letters in all, written from right to left. Depending on where a letter appears in a word initial, medial, final, or standalone it might take on many shapes.

The Arabic alphabet's letters are as follows:

ض (DAAD)	أ (ALIF)
ط (TAA)	ب (BA)
ظ (ZHA)	ت (THA)
ع (AIN)	ث (SA)
غ (GHAIN)	ج (JIM)
ف (FA)	ح (HA)
ق (QAF)	خ (KHA)
ك (KAF)	د (DAL)
ل (LAM)	ذ (DHAL)
م (MEEM)	ر (RA)
ن (NOON)	ز (ZAY)
ه (HA)	س (SEEN)
و (WAW)	ش (SHEEN)
ي (YA)	ص (SAD)

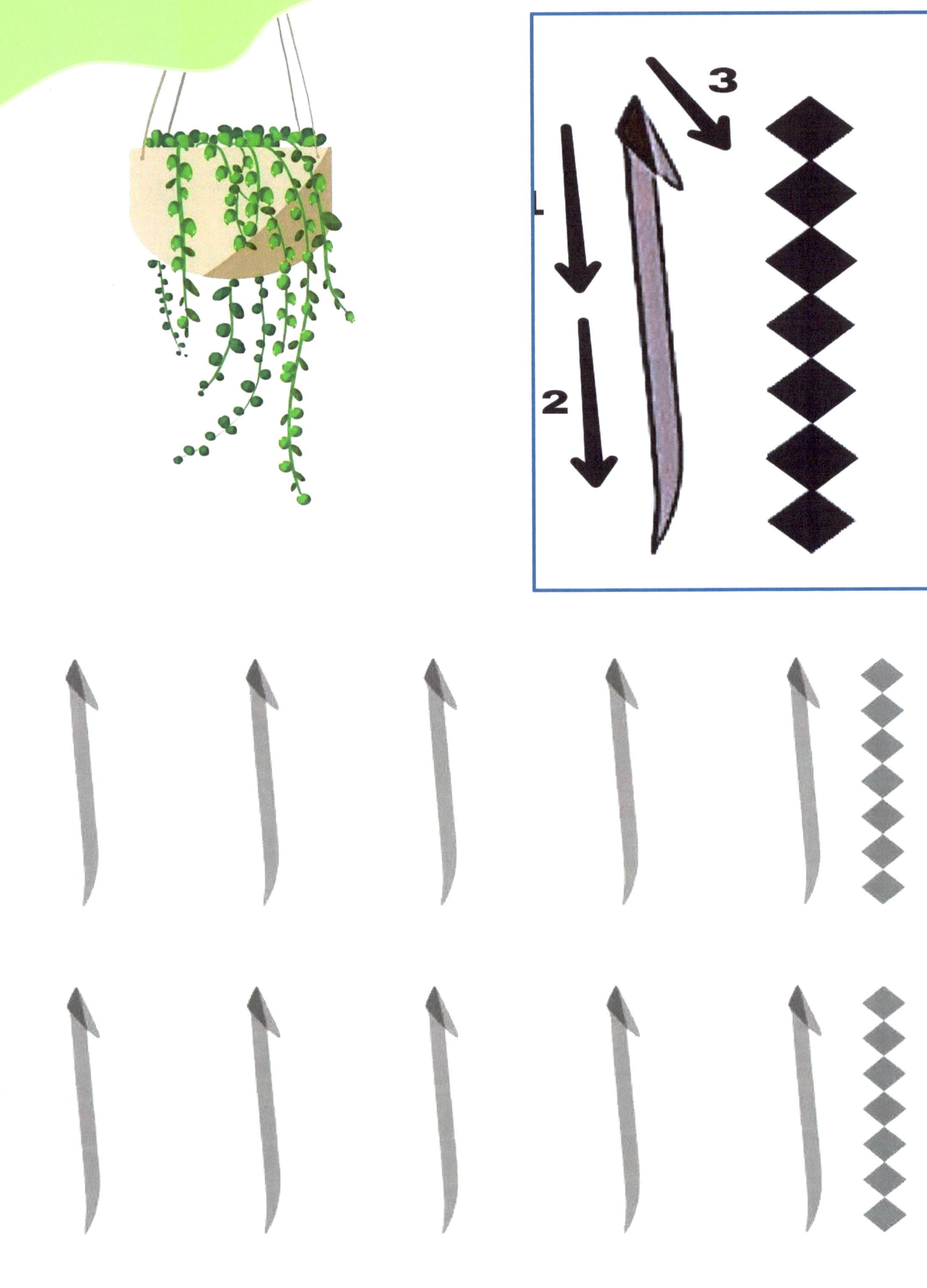

3
1
2

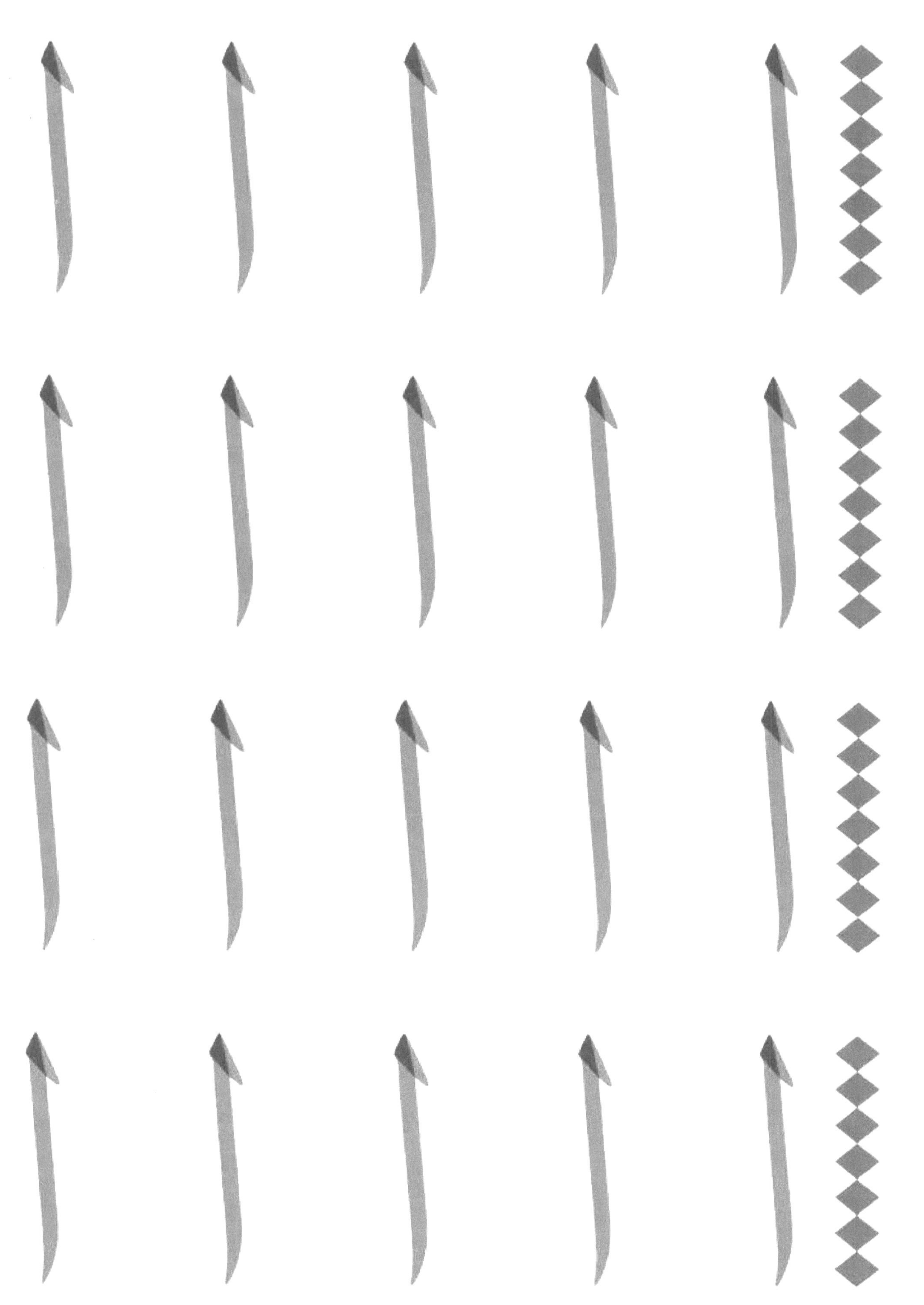

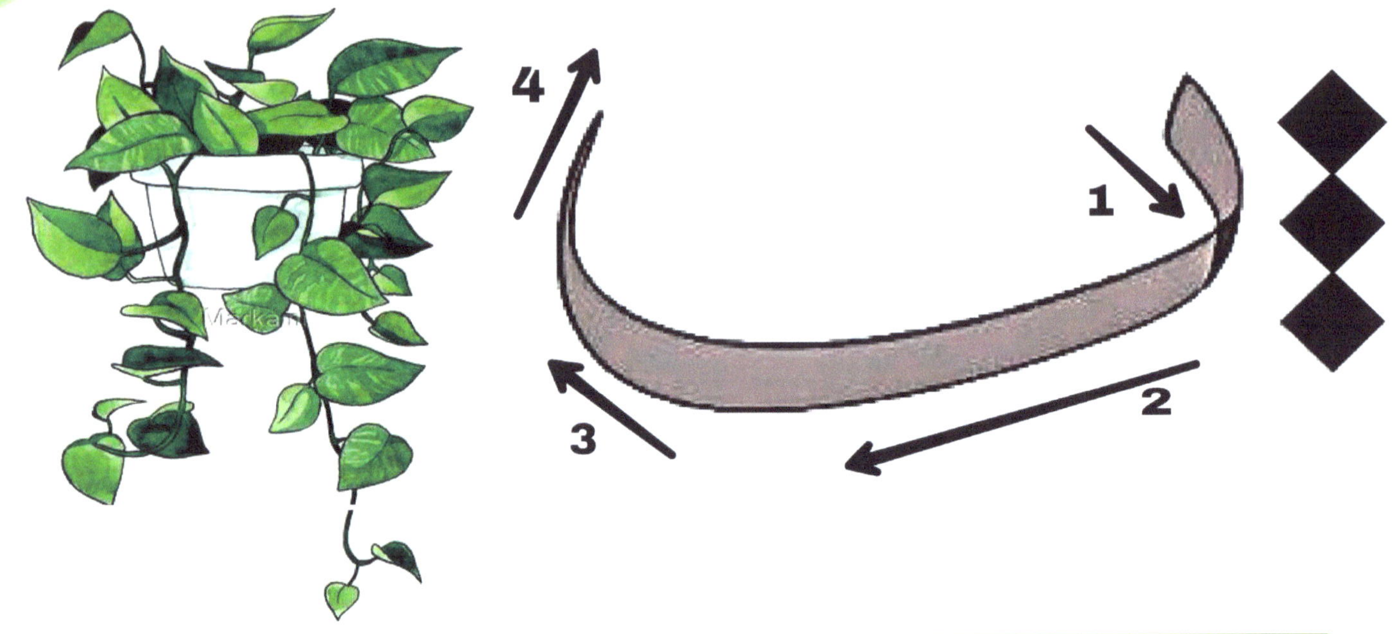

This stroke is used for ب ت ث

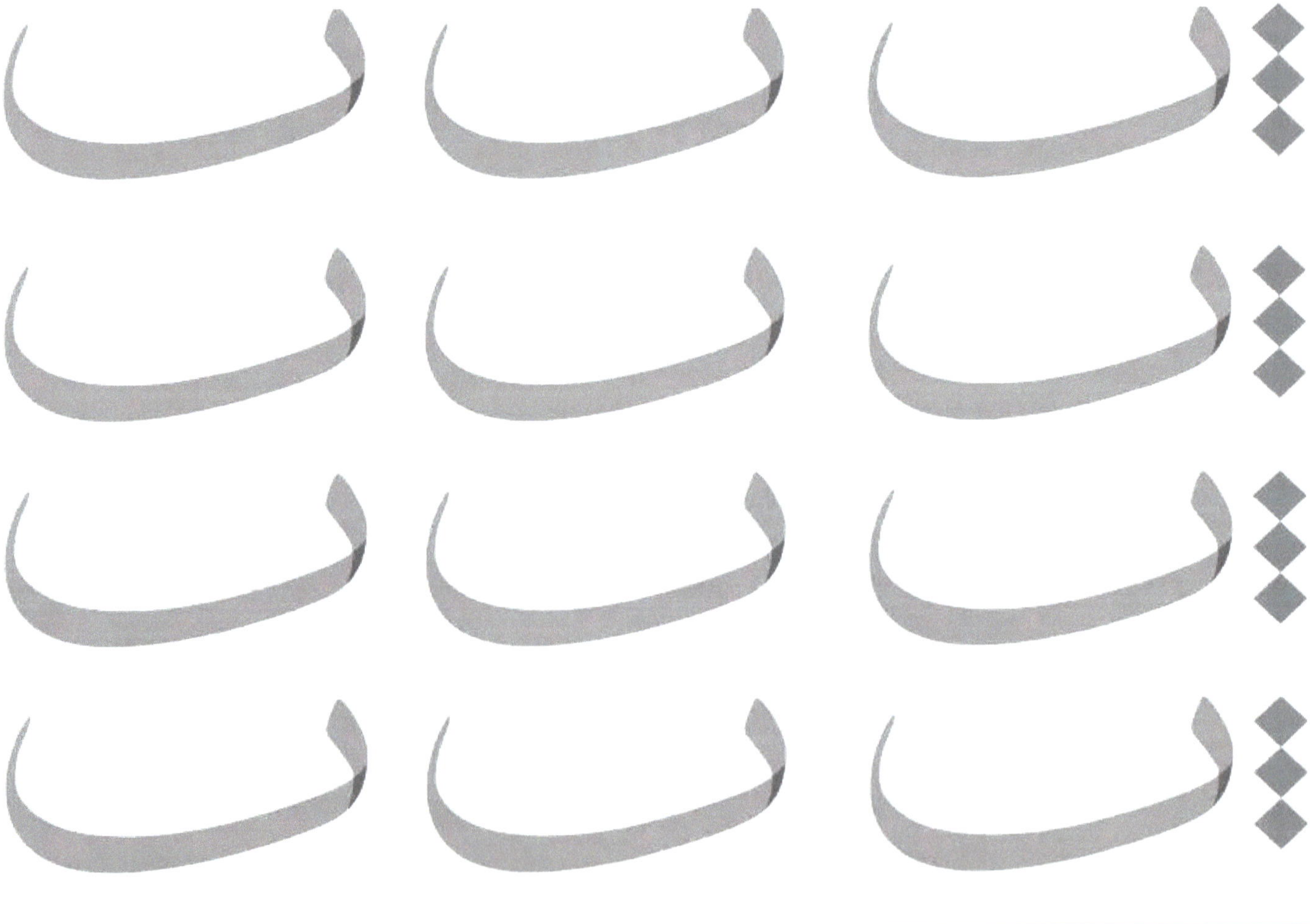

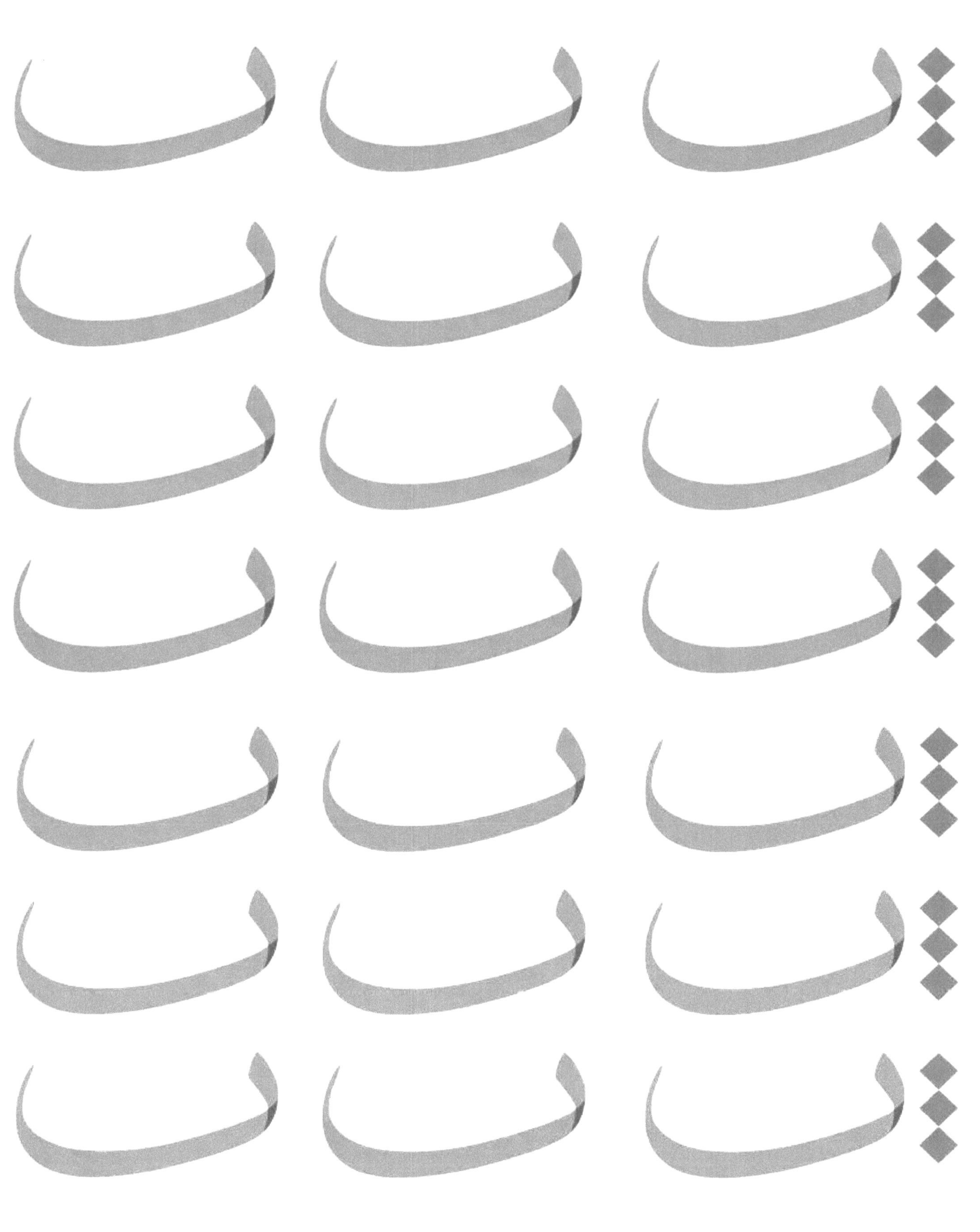

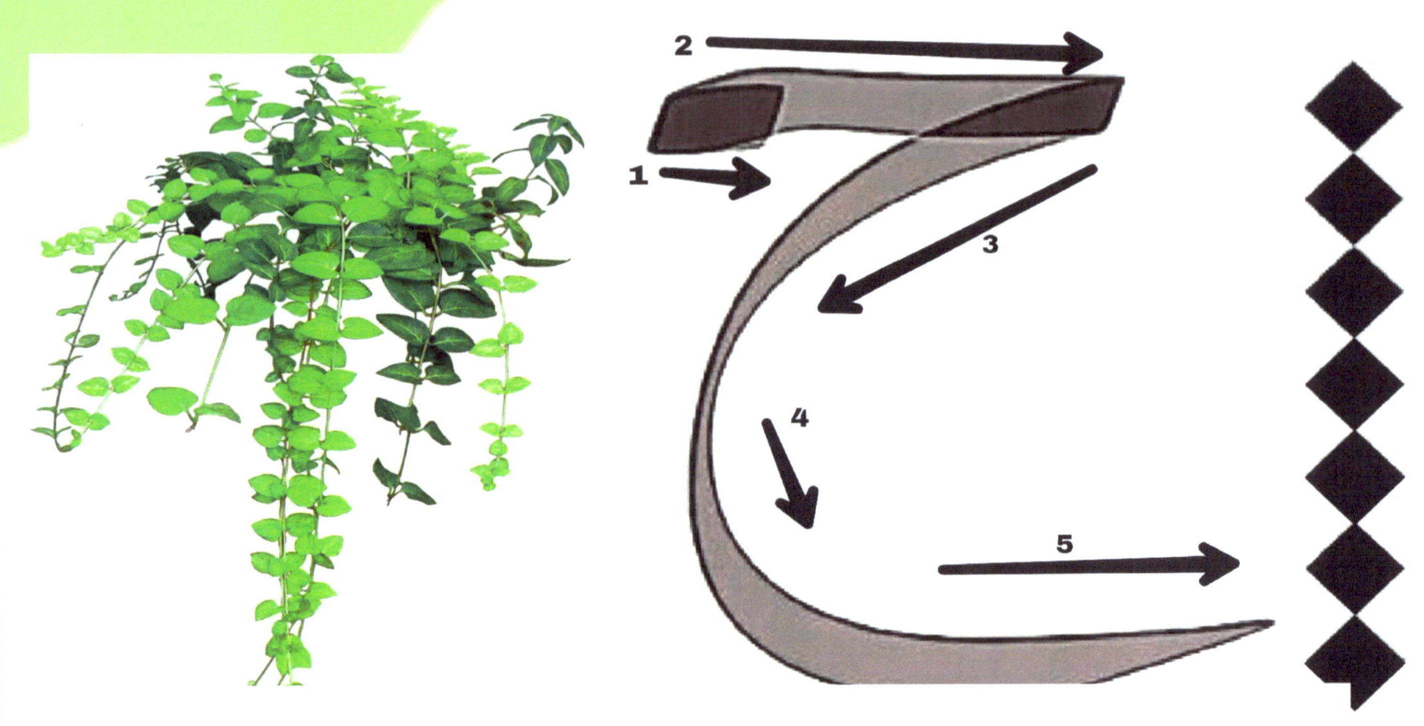

This stroke is used for خ ح ج

ح ح ح

ح ح ح

ح ح ح

ح ح ح

This stroke is used for د ذ

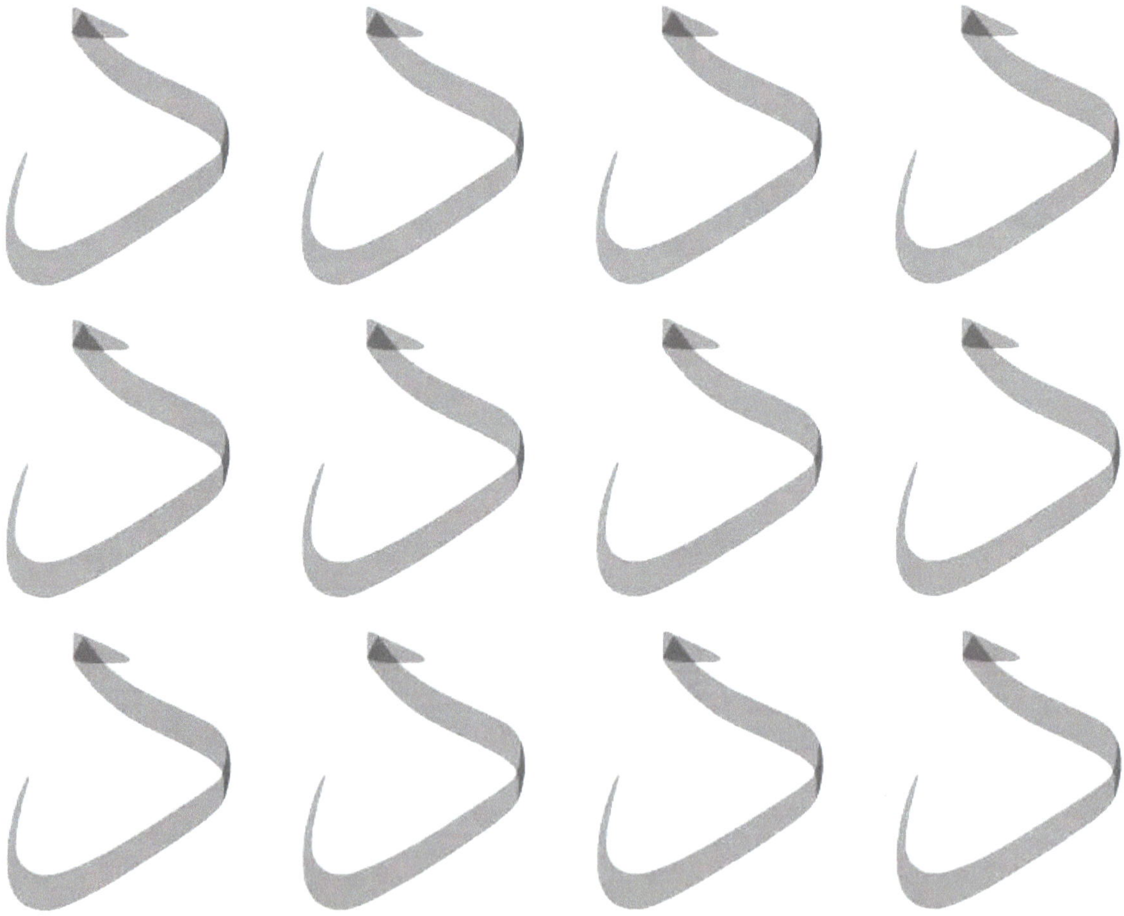

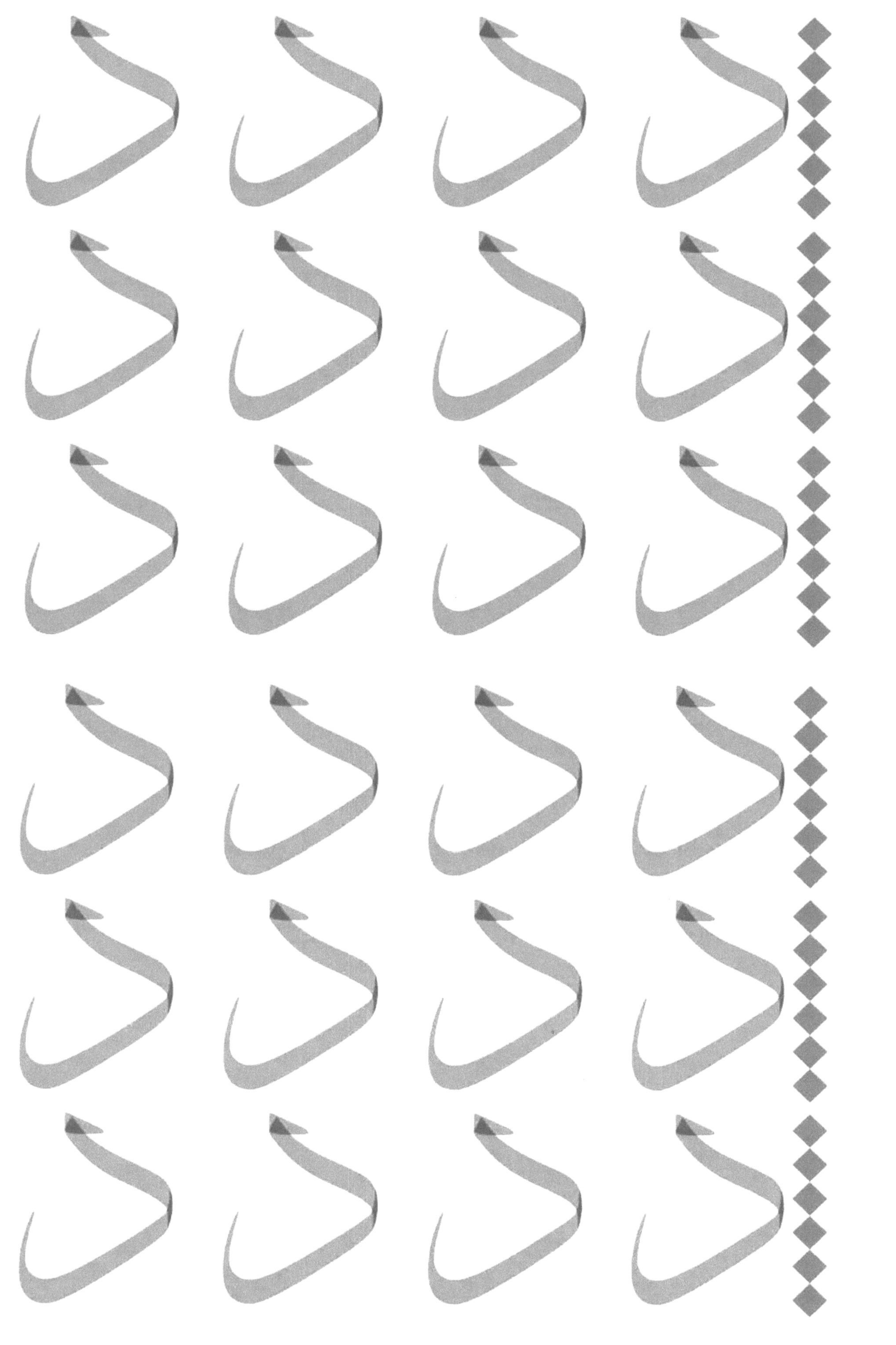

This stroke is used for ز ر

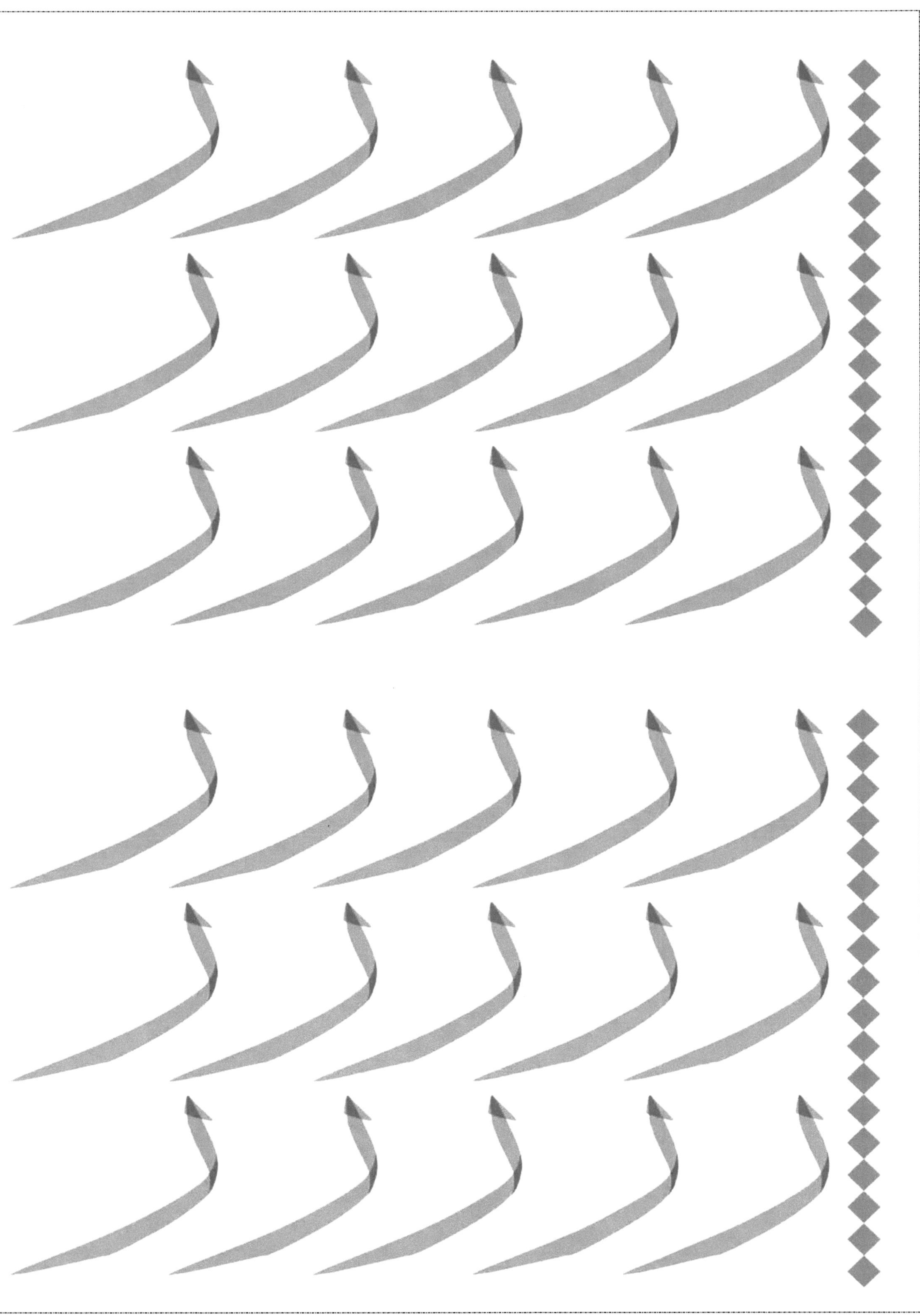

This stroke is used for ش س

س س س

س س س

س س س

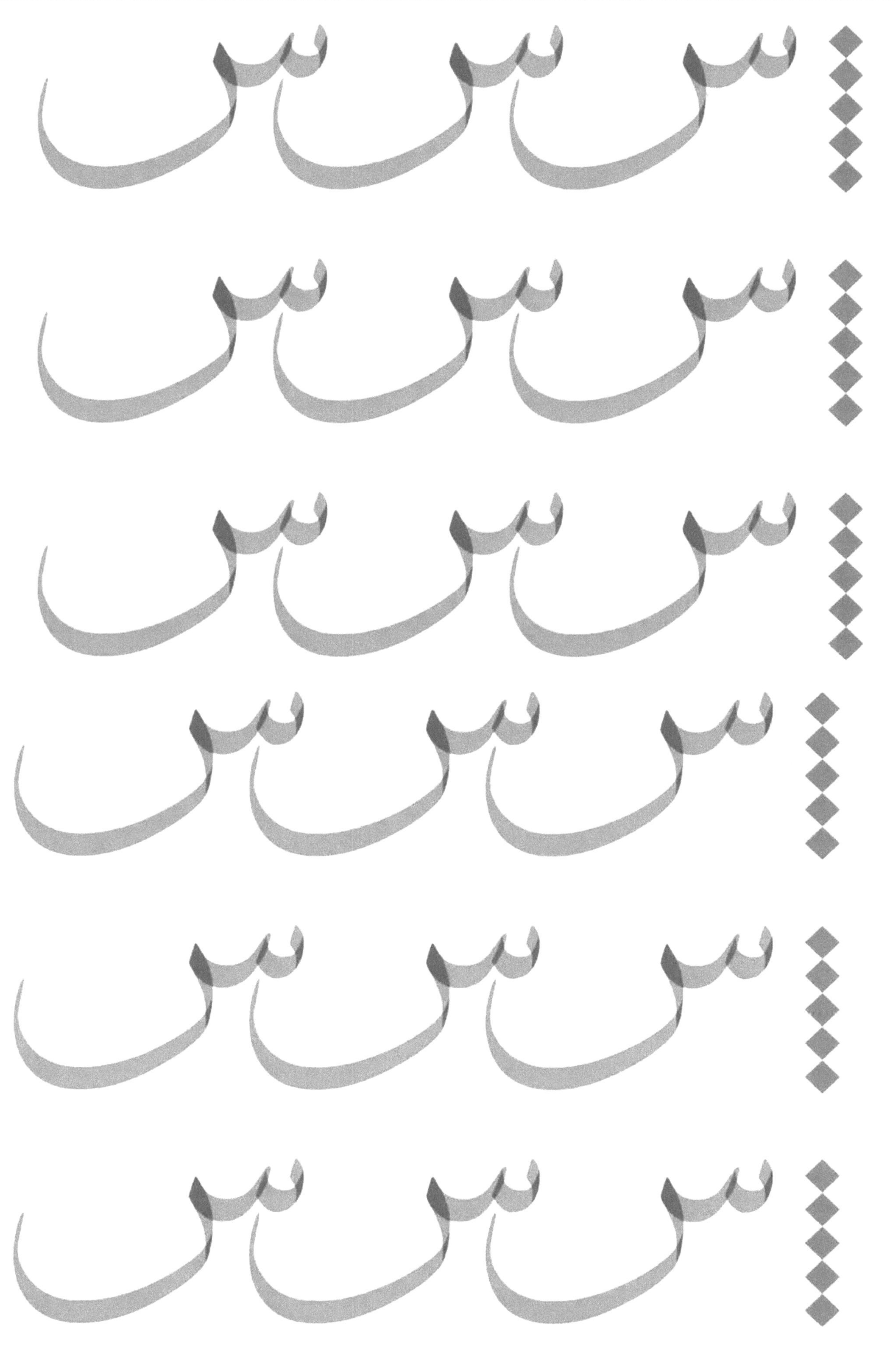

This stroke is used for ض ص

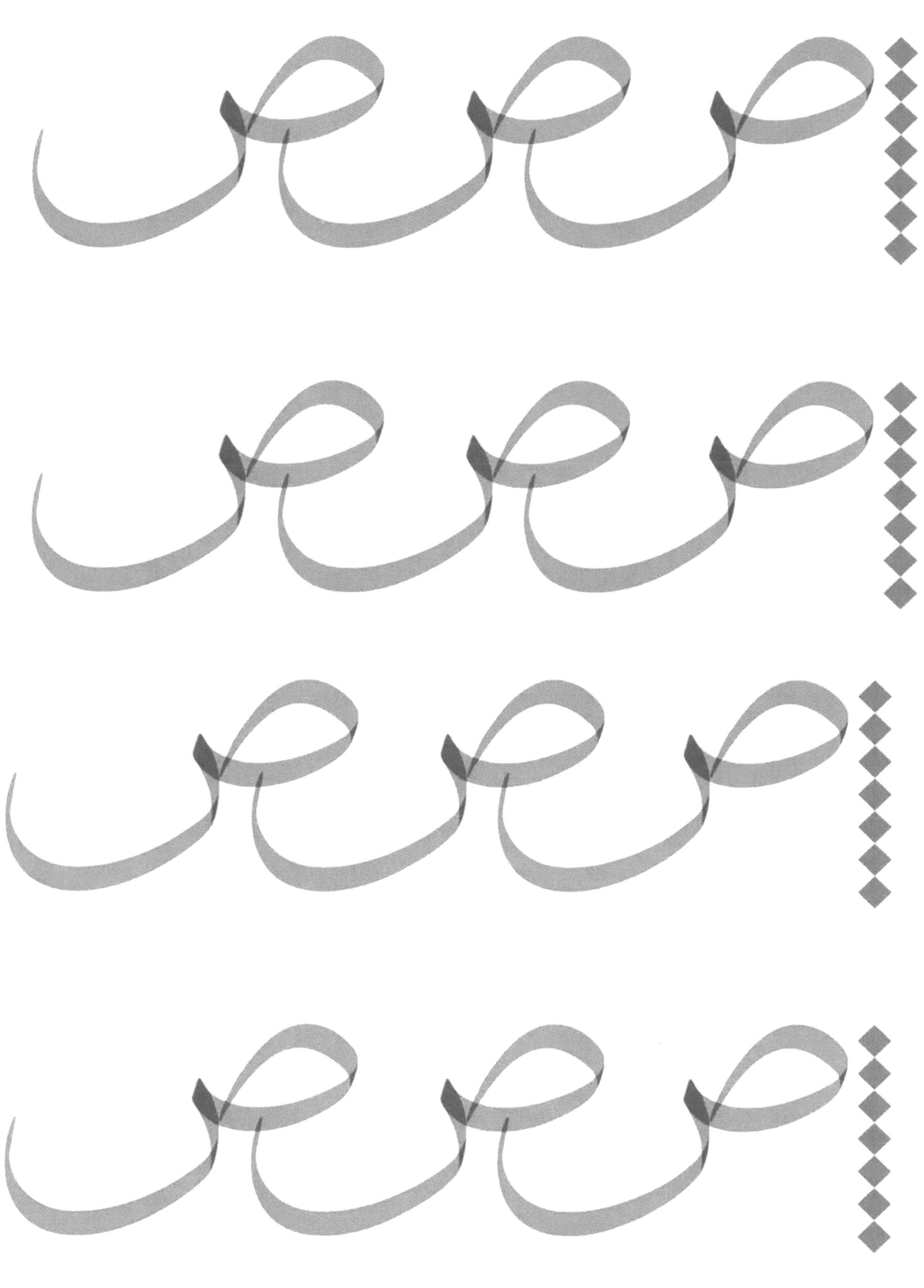

This stroke is used for ظ ط

ط ط ط ط

ط ط ط ط

ط ط ط ط

ط ط ط ط

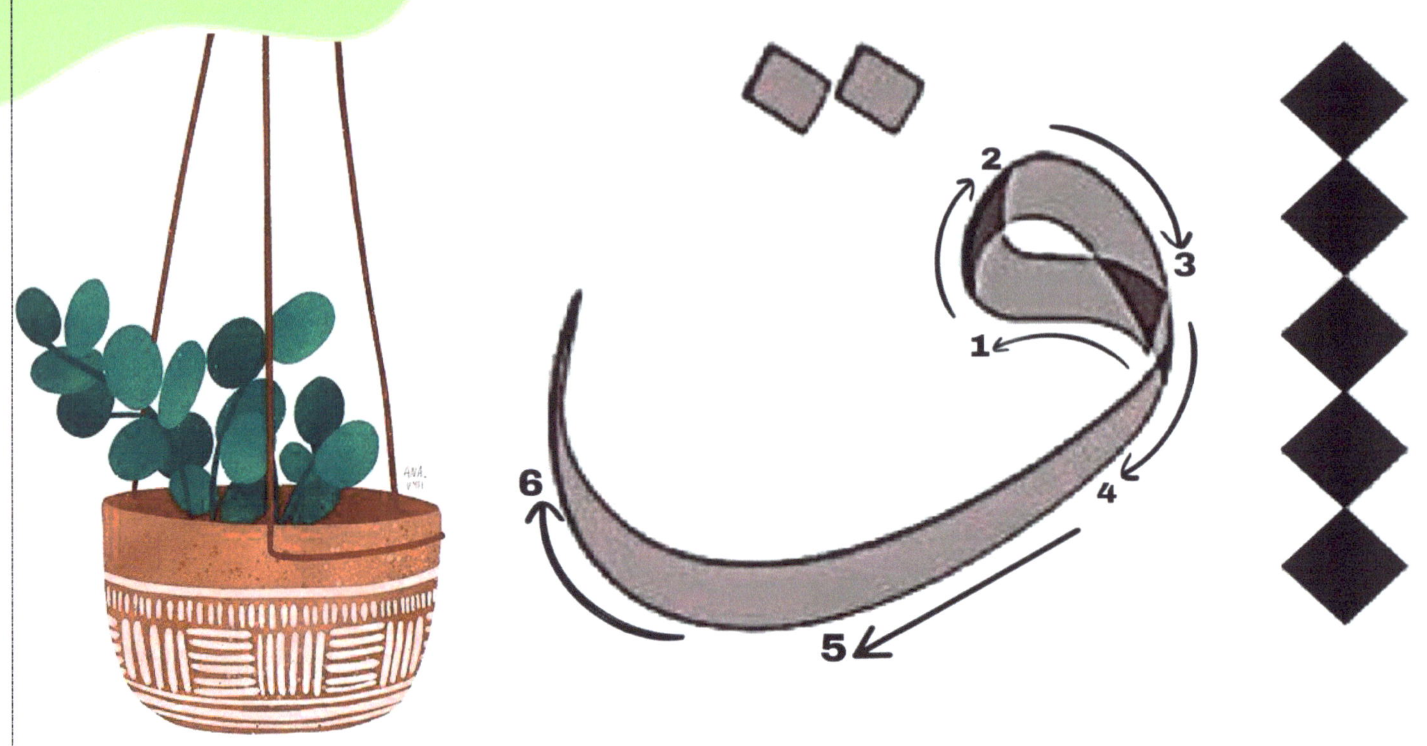

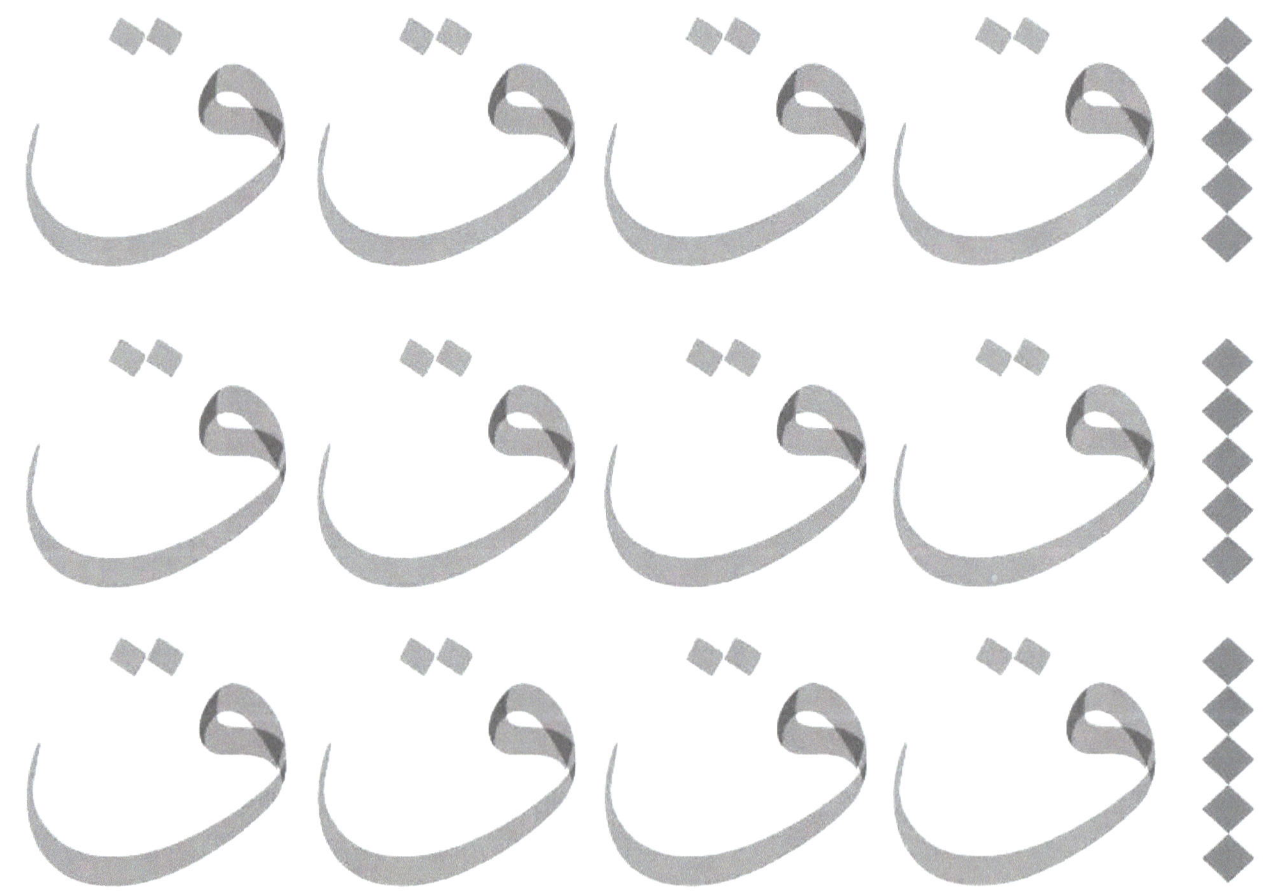

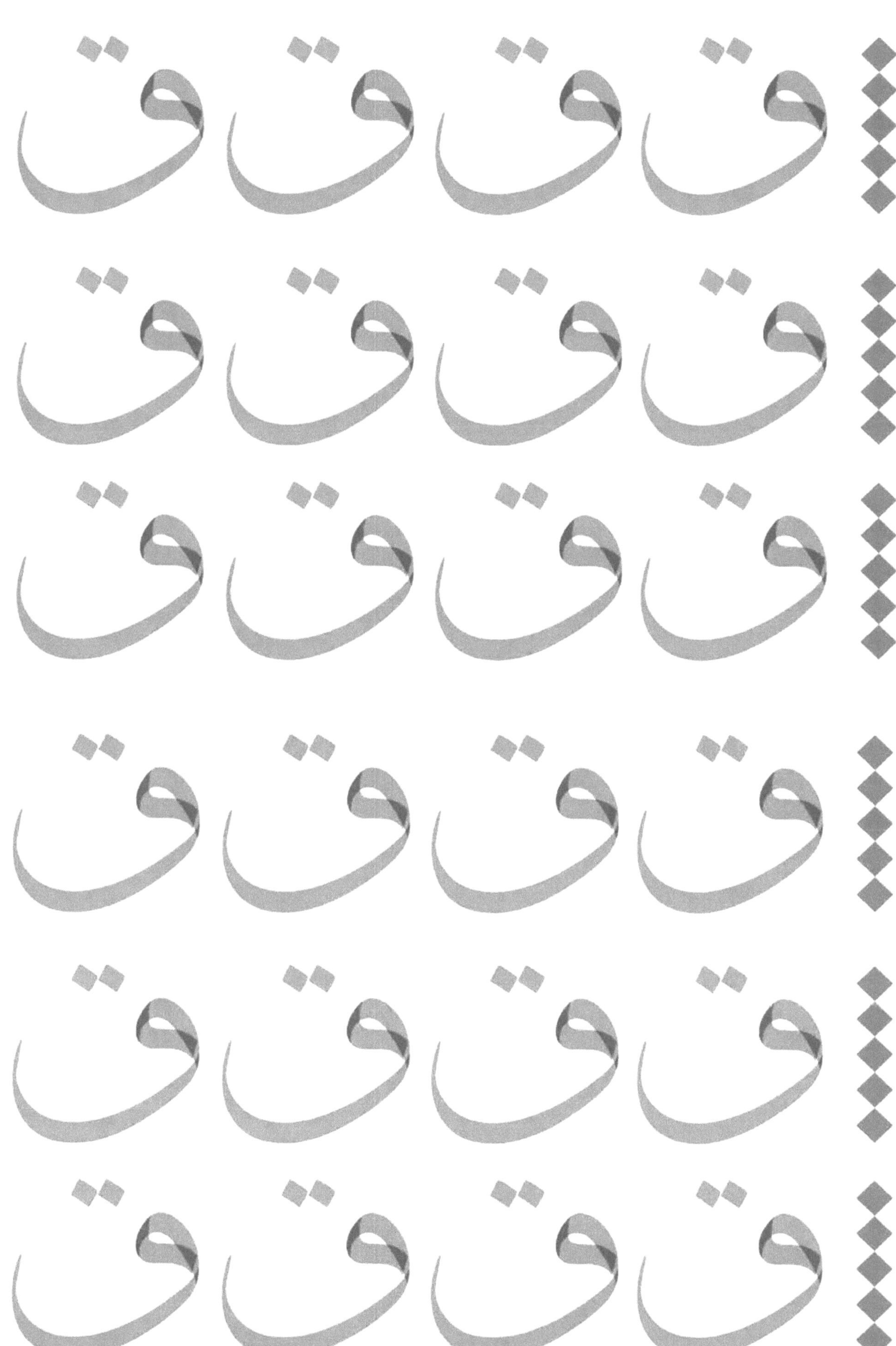

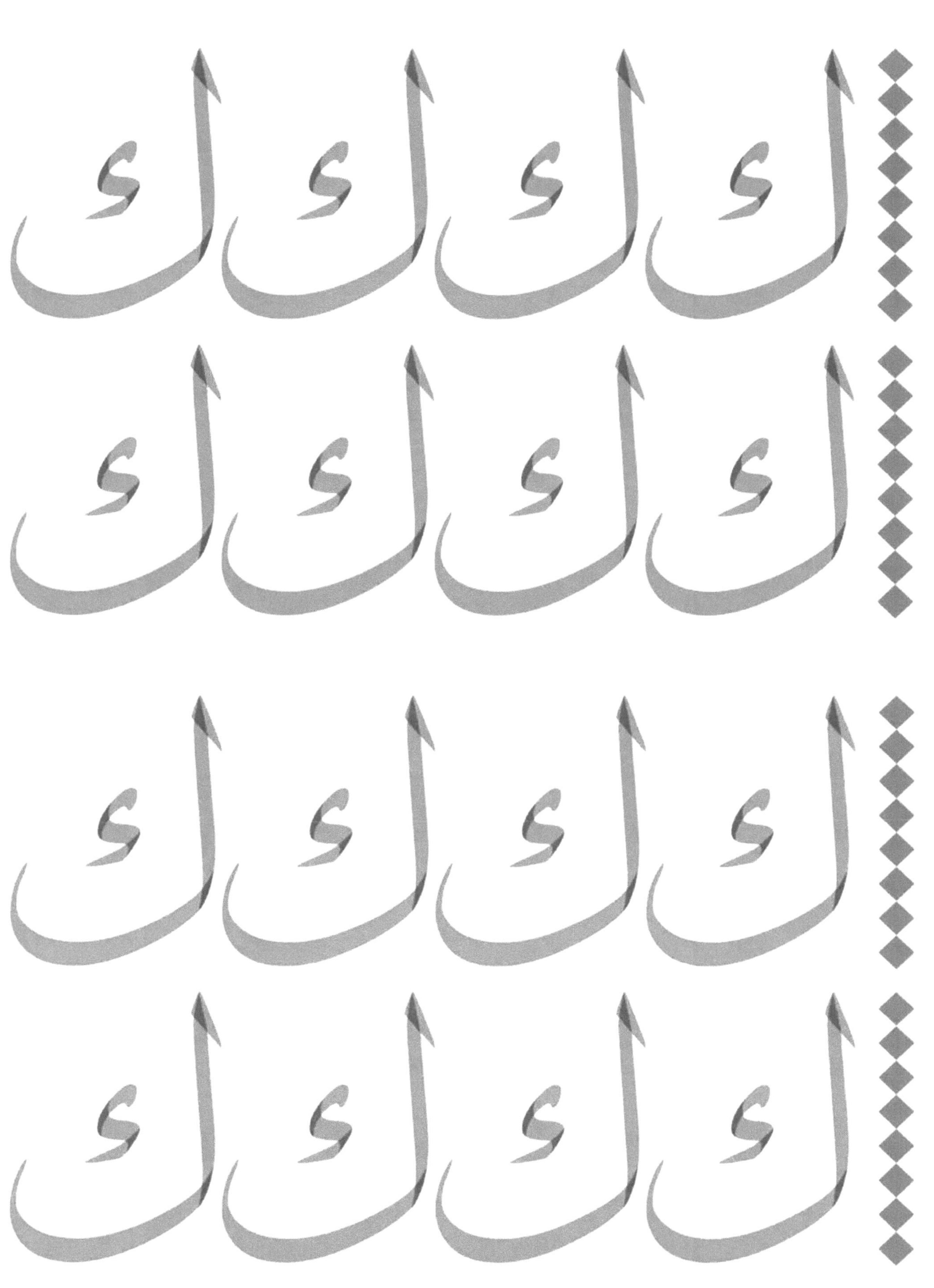

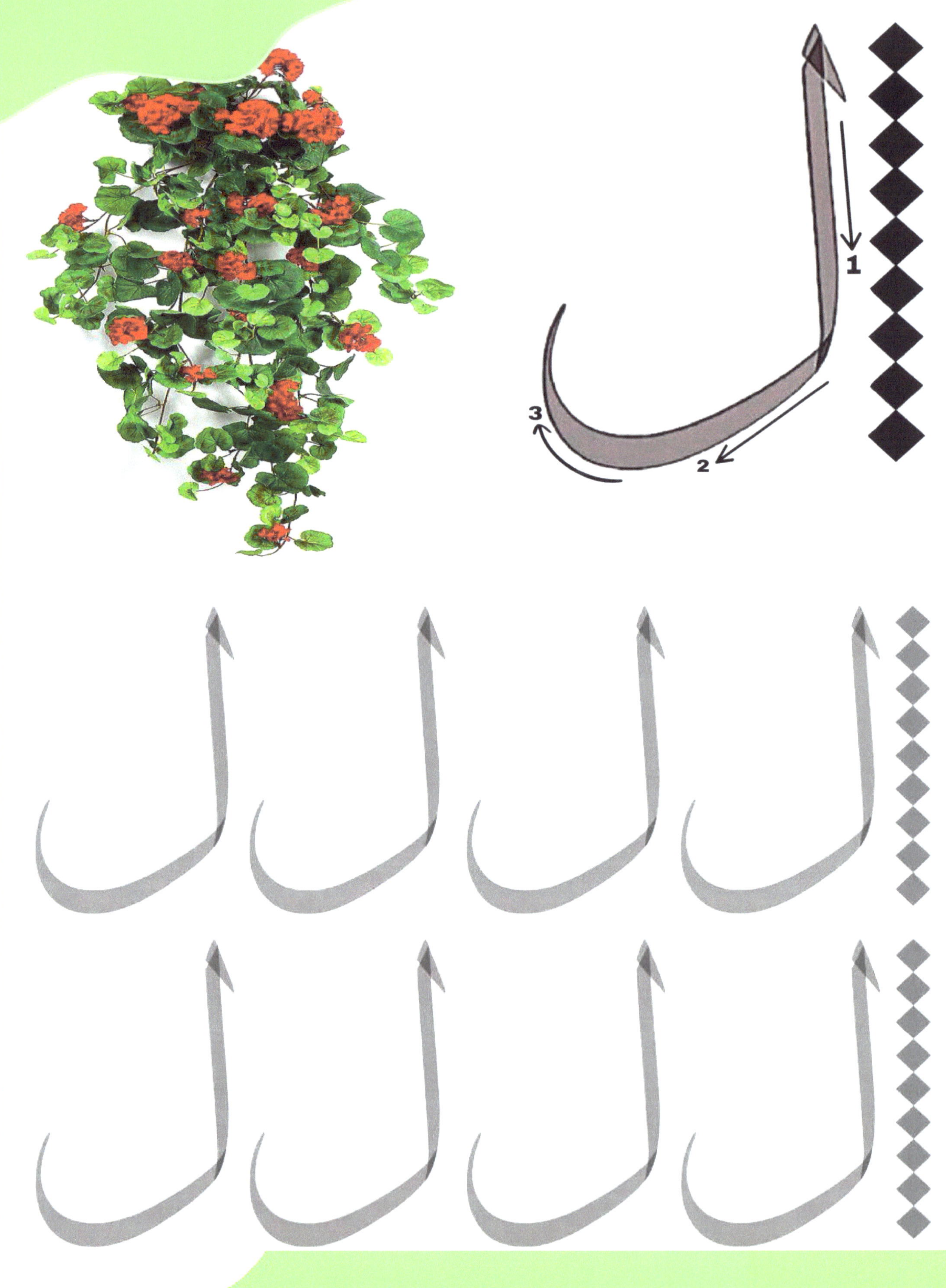

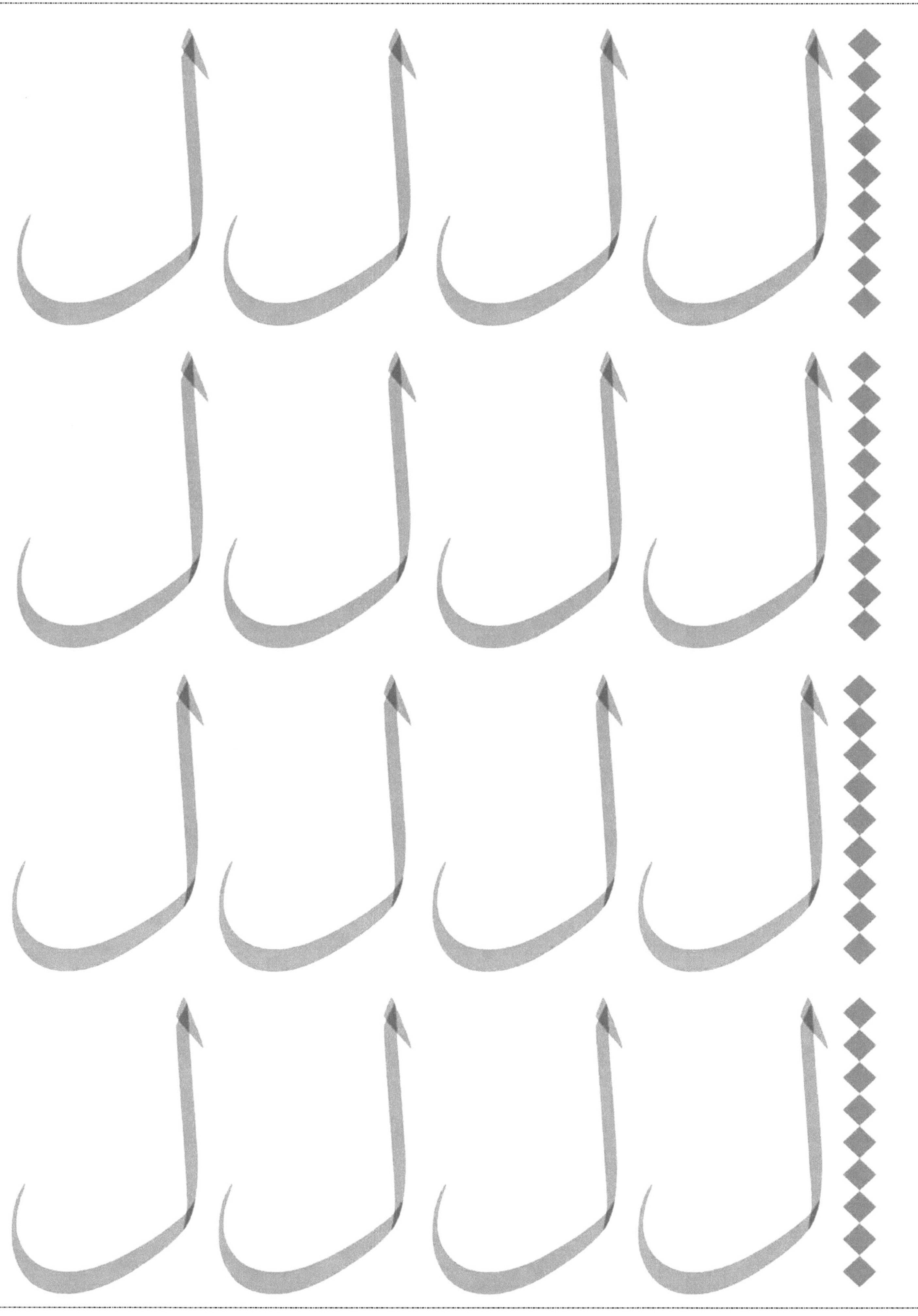

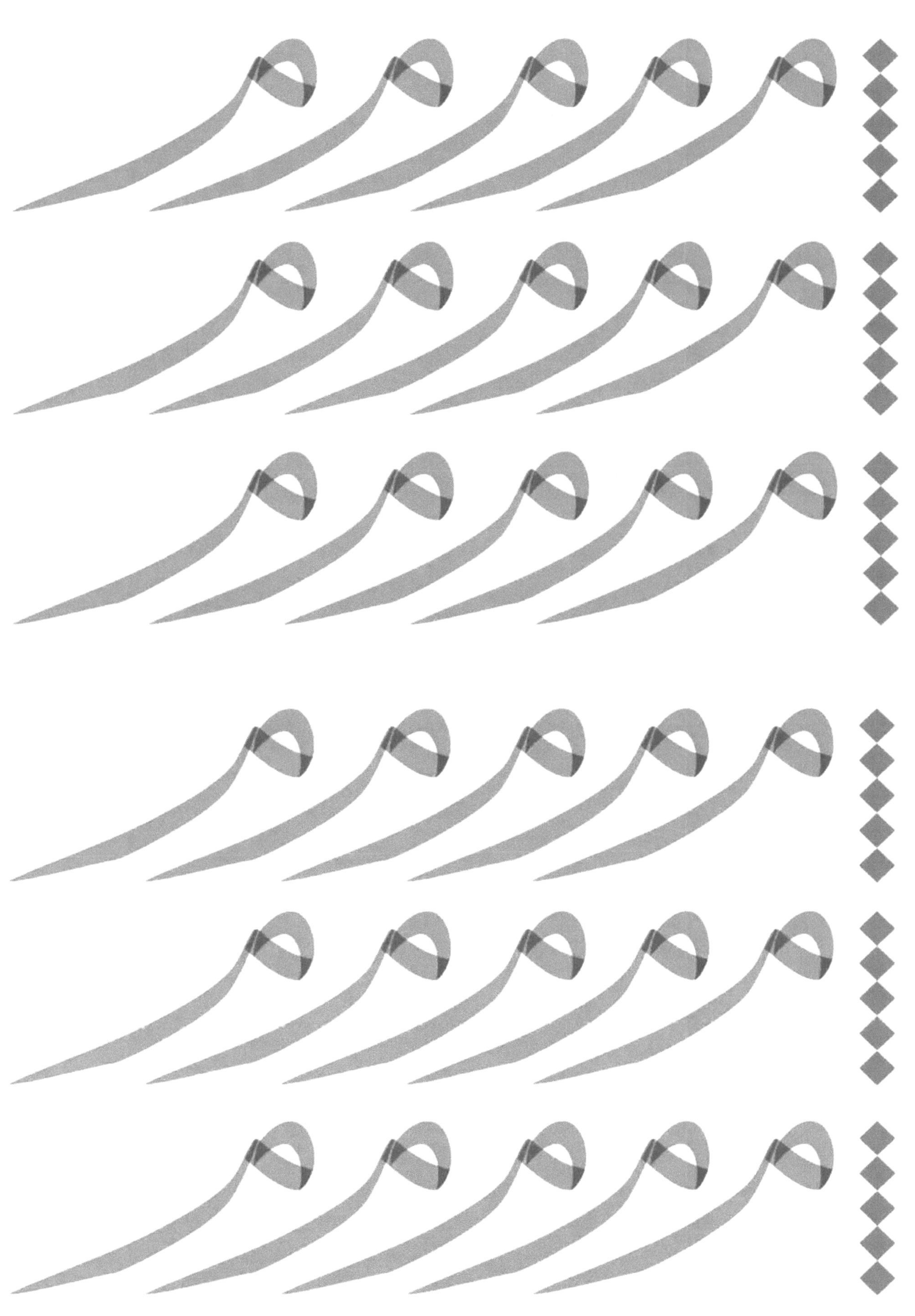

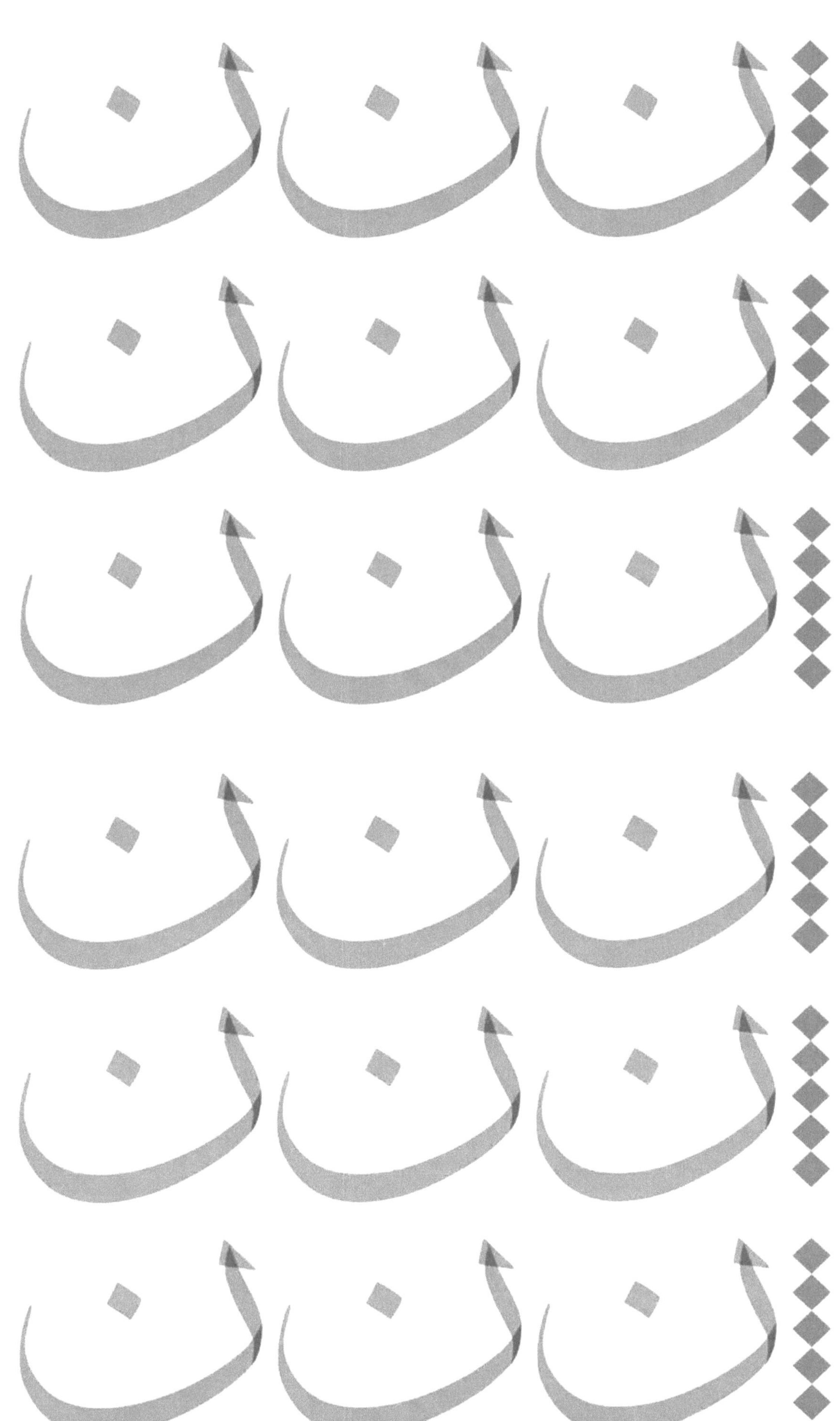

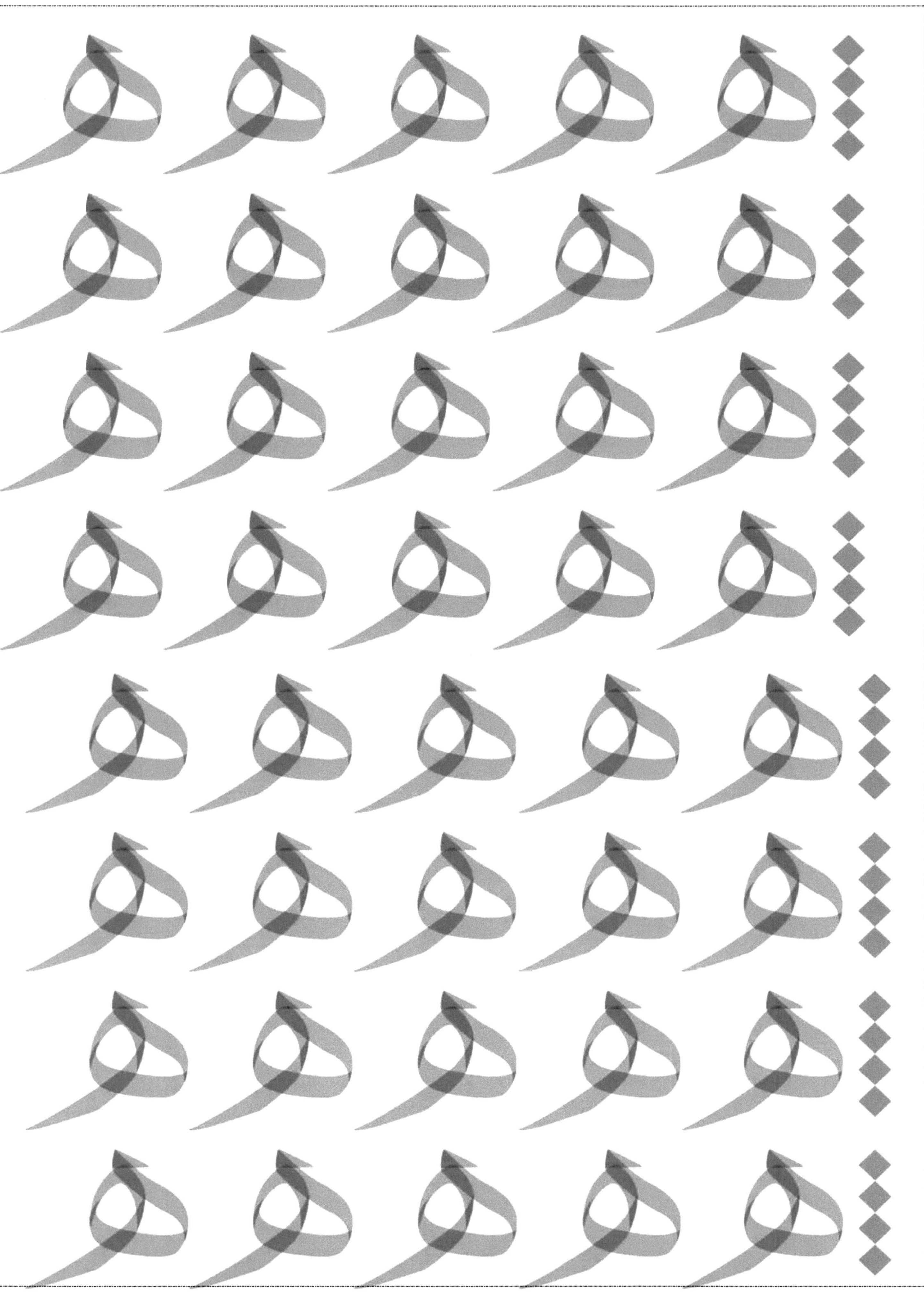